W9-CNG-259

**Bungalo Books**

**Illustrated by John Bianchi**
**Written by John Bianchi**
**© Copyright 1995 by Bungalo Books**

**Third printing 1997**

**Cataloguing in Publication Data**

Bianchi, John
    The toad sleeps over


ISBN 0-921285-41-8 (bound)        ISBN 0-921285-40-X (pbk.)


I. Title


PS8553.I26T63 1995      jC813'.54    C95-900513-7
PZ10.3.B43To 1995


Published in Canada by:              Trade Distribution:
Bungalo Books                       Firefly Books Ltd.
Ste.100                             3680 Victoria Park Ave.
17 Elk Court                        Willowdale, Ontario
Kingston, Ontario                   M2H 3K1
K7M 7A4

Co-published in U.S.A. by:           Printed in Canada by:
Firefly Books (U.S.) Inc.            Friesen Printers
Ellicott Station                    Altona, Manitoba
P.O. Box 1338                       ROG OBO
Buffalo, New York
14205

Visit Bungalo Books on the Net at:
*www.bungalobooks.com*

Send E-mail to Bungalo Books at:
*Bungalo@cgocable.net*

# The Toad Sleeps Over

## by John Bianchi

Monsanto, Myrtle and Minifield were sitting at the dinner table finishing the last of their berry-cup pudding when the doorbell rang. It was a cool, wet night, and Monsanto had planned to spend the rest of the evening reading quietly and snacking on a warm peanut.

But it was not to be.

"Ding," went the doorbell again.

"Ya-hoo," squealed little Minifield. "It's Tony!"

Monsanto looked at Myrtle.

"Who is Tony?" he asked darkly.

"Tony Bufo, dear," said Myrtle. "He's sleeping over tonight. That must be the Bufos dropping him off now."

"Why are they croaking?" Monsanto asked.

"Well, probably because they're toads," said Myrtle. "Croaking is what toads do."

As soon as Monsanto opened the door, little Tony Bufo burst in and knocked Monsanto's rare seed collection all over the floor.

"Sorry," croaked Tony as he and Minifield hopped upstairs.

"Would you like to come in?" Monsanto asked the toads.

"Nope!" burped Mr. Bufo. "There are lots of great bugs out tonight, so we're gonna get an early start on dinner."

With that, Mr. and Mrs. Bufo bounded off into the night, their big flat feet squishing and slapping with each step.

"I thought we were going to have a quiet evening," grumbled Monsanto as he closed the door.

"We will," said Myrtle. "We…"

Thump went the ceiling.

"What's going on up there?" demanded Monsanto.

"Tony's teaching me to hop!" called Minifield.

"I don't think that's a good idea," replied Monsanto, eyeing a crack in the ceiling. "You're wrecking the house!"

Turning to Myrtle, he protested, "I really don't think that Minifield should hang around with such ruffians. Toads can be so loud."

"Well, they are having fun," answered Myrtle as the two friends came racing down the stairs.

"Look at this," shouted Minifield.

"What's happened to your new harmonica?" exclaimed Myrtle.

"Tony slimed it," laughed Minifield. "Isn't it neat! Watch what it does when I play."

As Minifield began to play a tune, great, shiny bubbles of slime came oozing out of the harmonica.

"I think you should play that outside," said Monsanto sternly as he ushered the two youngsters out the door. He was beginning to lose his patience.

Monsanto had just mopped the slime off the kitchen floor, when Minifield burst back into the house.

"Tony showed me how to catch bugs," he announced, holding up a small ladybug.

"Isn't that interesting," said Myrtle.

"He does it with his tongue," giggled Minifield.

"Good heavens," muttered Monsanto.

Just then, Tony hopped into the room with an enormous dragonfly hanging out of his mouth.

"Let it go!" demanded Monsanto.

The dragonfly zoomed around the living room, sending newspapers, seeds and lampshades into the air.

"I didn't mean in here!" shouted Monsanto.

"Zap." Tony's tongue flashed out and stuck to the dragonfly. As his tongue recoiled, the insect snapped back into the little toad's mouth.

"Cool," Minifield squealed.

"Take it out of the house, and let it go," Monsanto commanded, almost exploding with anger. "NOW!"

"That's it," he complained when the door closed. "The toad will NOT sleep over!"

Monsanto stormed off to get his raincoat and galoshes.

"But, dear, you'll hurt Tony's feelings," fretted Myrtle. "And besides, there won't be anyone home."

"I'll find those toads along the way," said Monsanto, heading out the door.

Outside, the falling rain pelted Monsanto's face and dripped off his whiskers as he scanned the yard for Minifield and Tony. Finally, he spotted their tracks leading toward the stream. It was raining harder now, and this made him even angrier as he started off after them.

Suddenly, his heart skipped a beat. There was a third set of footprints in the muddy path — coyote tracks!

Monsanto ran as fast as his legs could carry him. If the youngsters were following the trail that led down to the stream, he could take the shortcut and, with some luck, save them from the coyote.

It didn't take long to find them.

"Come here quickly!" shouted Monsanto. But Minifield and Tony did not have time. A large coyote leapt from the shadows and, with a low, rumbling growl, started inching toward them.

"Run!" called Monsanto, feeling more helpless by the second.

But Minifield was too frightened to move. Trembling with fear, he started to cry.

"Relax," croaked Tony. And with that, he flicked out his long, wet tongue and slapped the coyote right in the middle of its eye.

"Yeoww!" howled the coyote. Furious, it lunged and snatched up poor Tony in its mouth.

"Stop!" yelled Monsanto.

"No need to worry about me," Tony called down to him. "Don't forget that I'm a toad." And before the coyote had a chance to bite down, Tony inflated himself to three times his normal size.

"Aaaahhh," cried the coyote, its mouth jammed open.

"Cool," gasped Minifield.

"Tony, I think you had better come down," cried Monsanto.

"Okay," Tony called cheerfully. "I just have to teach this critter the three Ts: Toads Taste Terrible."

That said, the young toad opened the glands at the side of his head and gave the coyote a large dose of toad venom.

The coyote's eyes went scarlet and swirled in their sockets. Sweat poured from its brow. White wisps of steam gushed from its ears. With a tremendous cough, it spit Tony into the air, dashed down to the stream and plunged into the water.

As the trio watched from the riverbank, the coyote ran into the night, sputtering and howling under the clearing sky.

U pon their return home, the youngsters told Myrtle of their escapade while she listened in amazement. Then she sent them straight to the bathtub where Tony taught Minifield how to croak.

Later, in the kitchen, Minifield carefully recorded every detail of their exciting encounter in his journal while Myrtle served everyone hot chocolate with marshmallows on top.

Monsanto doted on Minifield and Tony for the rest of the evening. His attitude toward toads had clearly undergone a remarkable change. At bedtime, he insisted upon reading them a book, but the pair fell asleep within minutes.

The next morning, when Mr. and Mrs. Bufo came by to pick up Tony, Monsanto invited them to stay for coffee. They all sat out on the deck where everyone had a wonderful time sipping their drinks and discussing the night's adventure.

Monsanto even let Mr. Bufo teach him how to catch bugs with his tongue.

# The Author and Illustrator

John Bianchi is a cartoonist, illustrator and author who divides his time between his studio in Arizona's Sonoran Desert, where he lives with his family, and Bungalo World Headquarters in eastern Ontario. A well-known magazine illustrator, he co-founded Bungalo Books in 1986 and has created 30 children's books to date.

*John can be reached on the Internet at: bungalo@cgocable.net*

## Official Bungalo Reading Buddies

Kids who love to read books are eligible to become official, card-carrying Bungalo Reading Buddies. If you and your friends want to join an international club dedicated to having fun while reading, show this notice to your teacher or librarian. We'll send your class a great membership kit.

## Teachers and Librarians

Bungalo Books would be pleased to send you a Reading Buddy membership kit that includes 30 full-colour, laminated membership cards. These pocket-sized, 2¼-by-4-inch membership cards can be incorporated into a wide variety of school and community reading programmes for primary, junior and intermediate elementary school students.

✳ **Each kit includes 30 membership cards, postcards, bookmarks, a current Bungalo Reading Buddy newsletter and a Bungalo storybook.**
✳ **Kits cost only $7.50 for postage and handling.**
✳ **No cash please. Make cheque or money order payable to Bungalo Books.**
✳ **Offer limited to libraries and schools.**
✳ **Please allow four weeks for delivery.**

**Bungalo World Headquarters**
**17 Elk Court**
**Suite 100**
**Kingston, Ontario**
**K7M 7A4**